THE ZACK FILES

How to Speak Dolphin in Three Easy Lessons

For Judith, and for the real Zack,
with love—D.G.

THE ZACK FILES™

How to Speak Dolphin in Three Easy Lessons

By Dan Greenburg

Illustrated by Jack E. Davis

GROSSET & DUNLAP • NEW YORK

I'd like to thank my editors,
Jane O'Connor and Judy Donnelly,
who make the process of writing and revising
so much fun, and without whom
these books would not exist.

I also want to thank
Jennifer Dussling and Laura Driscoll
for their terrific ideas.

Text copyright © 1997 by Dan Greenburg. Illustrations copyright © 1997 by Jack E. Davis. All rights reserved. Published by Grosset & Dunlap, Inc., a division of Penguin Putnam Books for Young Readers, New York. THE ZACK FILES is a trademark of The Putnam & Grosset Group. GROSSET & DUNLAP is a trademark of Grosset & Dunlap, Inc. Published simultaneously in Canada. Printed in the U.S.A.

Library of Congress Cataloging-in-Publication Data
Greenburg, Dan.
    How to speak dolphin in three easy lessons / by Dan Greenburg ; illustrated by Jack E. Davis.
    p.   cm. – (The Zack files)
    Summary: When Zack goes to Florida to visit Mel & Shirley's Wonderful World of Dolphins, he is surprised to discover that he can understand and speak to dolphins, which enables him to solve a kidnapping.
    [1. Dolphins–Fiction. 2. Human-animal communication–Fiction. 3. Florida–Fiction.]   I. Davis, Jack E., ill. II. Title. III. Series: Greenburg, Dan. Zack files.
PZ7.G8278Ho 1997
[Fic]–dc21   97-38285
                                                                                                    CIP
                                        2004 Printing   AC
ISBN 0-448-41736-7

Chapter 1

I have to ask you something. How smart do you think dolphins are? I always figured they were somewhere between chimpanzees and NFL linebackers. Then I had a weird experience with dolphins that totally changed my mind.

Not that having weird experiences is a big deal to me. Once a volcano goddess in Hawaii put a curse on me. Another time a bratty girl ghost named Wanda trashed our apartment. And I also met a boy who turned out to be my son from the future.

He was on a time tour bus with his school class. Stuff like that.

Oh, by the way, my name is Zack. I'm ten and a half, and I go to the Horace Hyde-White School for Boys in New York City. There aren't a whole lot of dolphins here. The dolphins I met lived in Florida. My dad and I drove down there over spring vacation.

My dad is a freelance writer. That means he works at home, sitting at his desk all day and staring out the window. He calls that "roughing out ideas." People give him money for it. When I do it in school they call it "not paying attention." People give me detention for it.

Anyway, getting back to Florida. Dad was going there to write an article for *Fruit Growers' Digest* about the world's largest orange. This orange was about the size of a basketball. That's bigger than the ones we usually get at our supermarket in New York

City. The town where they grew this orange was near a tiny motel and amusement park called Mel & Shirley's Wonderful World of Dolphins. We were staying there because Mel and Shirley are really old friends of my Grandma Leah.

It seemed like the trip was never going to end. Finally we turned off the turnpike onto a smaller road. In five more minutes we were there. On the roof of the motel was this neon sign in the shape of a smiling dolphin. The words "Four Shows Daily" blinked on and off in the neon waterspout above the neon dolphin's head.

Near the motel there was a little roller-coaster track with only two tiny bumps in it. It wouldn't have even scared a baby, but they called it the Screamer. There were some kiddie rides with cars in the shape of dolphins. And, of course, they had this big dolphin pool.

Mel and Shirley were playing a game of Scrabble by the dolphin pool.

"We've been waiting for you," said Shirley. She came right over and began kissing me and Dad all over the place.

Dad took our bags out of the car. But Mel brushed Dad away and took them from him.

"Mel, I can carry those," said Dad.

"Get out of here," said Mel. "You think I'm an old man or something?"

They put our stuff in one of the little motel cabins. Then we all went into the front office so Shirley could give us a snack before bedtime.

On the walls were all kinds of framed photographs of Shirley with Mel in a pool. They were horsing around with two tiny dolphins.

"These are pictures of Ralph and Fluffy when they were babies," said Shirley. "Aren't they adorable?" I said they were.

Ralph and Fluffy are their dolphins. I personally doubt I'd name a dolphin Fluffy. I mean what's fluffy about a dolphin? Nothing, that's what. Later Dad told me that Fluffy was the name of a favorite cat of Shirley's that had died. So I guess that explains it. Except maybe not.

"Zack, would you like to meet Ralph and Fluffy?" Shirley asked.

"I'd love to," I said.

Shirley took me back outside to the edge of the dolphin pool. There were bleachers around it like at Sea World, only a lot smaller. It was pretty dark out, but you could see Ralph and Fluffy swimming round and round.

"Ralph! Fluffy!" Shirley called. "Come on, kids. Say hello to Zack!"

Both dolphins stopped swimming. They stuck their heads out of the water and made these really funny noises. Whistles

and sort of clicks: **K-K-K-K-K-K-K**. Then they waved their flippers at me.

Cool! This was the first time I'd seen real live dolphins and not on some TV nature show.

"Very nice, kids!" cried Shirley. "Very nice! Zack, throw them some treats."

Shirley handed me a bucket. It was filled with dead fish.

"Go ahead," said Shirley.

I wasn't crazy about touching dead fish, I really wasn't. But I also didn't want to be rude. I reached into the bucket, grabbed two slimy dead fish, and threw them into the pool. The dolphins caught them in their mouths and gulped them down.

"Very nice, kids!" cried Shirley.

"Krick, krick!" the dolphins chirped. They looked very pleased with themselves.

One of the dolphins swam right up to the edge of the pool. It waved at me again with

its flipper. So I waved back. It was the only polite thing to do. Then, I can't be absolutely sure of this, but it looked like it winked at me! Can dolphins wink? I was going to ask Dad about that. But I was too sleepy.

When I woke up the next morning, Dad had already left to interview the world's largest orange. Well, actually the guy who grew it. I told Dad I wanted to hang out at the motel anyway. Ralph and Fluffy were doing their first show at 10 A.M. I got to the dolphin pool a little early to get a good seat. I didn't have to rush. Besides Mel, I was the only person in the audience.

"Ladies and gentlemen," Shirley said into a microphone, "welcome to Mel and Shirley's Wonderful World of Dolphins. Let's have a big round of applause for the stars of our show—Ralph and Fluffy!"

I clapped very hard. So did Mel. I guess

that counted as a round of applause, because out swam Ralph and Fluffy.

Shirley had the dolphins do a whole lot of tricks. They did somersaults in the air. They swam on their backs. They tossed a basketball into a net. Michael Jordan didn't have anything to worry about. But they were pretty good for amateurs.

"Would somebody in the audience like to give Fluffy a hug?" Shirley asked. She looked around, like there was this big crowd. "How about you, young man?" she said, pointing to me.

"Uh, well, sure," I said. "I guess so."

I came down from the bleachers to the edge of the pool.

"Good," said Shirley. "Lean over the side of the pool. Make a big circle with your arms. Fluffy will rise up into the circle, and you'll hug her."

"OK," I said.

"Make the circle with your arms now."

"Like this?"

"Yep. Now lean over the side of the pool."

Fluffy rose right up into my arms. She put her head on my shoulder. I hugged her. It was a nice feeling. She felt like rubber. Smooth, wet, silver rubber.

Suddenly, I lost my balance and fell into the pool.

Kersplash!

Before I knew it, I was underwater. The water was freezing cold. But I happen to be a pretty good swimmer. So even with my clothes and shoes on, I was OK.

Suddenly I felt something underneath me. Pushing me upward. Pushing me to the surface. That's when the weird thing happened. This soft voice that wasn't mine sounded inside my head: **"I've got you, dear—you're safe."**

Then my head was out of the water. A second later I scrambled out of the pool.

"Zack, are you all right?" yelled Mel.

"Sure," I said. "A little wet is all."

About a thousand gallons of water poured off me.

"Are you really OK, Zack?" Shirley asked.

"Of course," I said, emptying my sneakers. "But you want to hear something weird? When I was underwater, I think Fluffy talked to me."

"Well, of *course* she talked to you," said Shirley. "She whistles. She clicks. She makes all kinds of sounds."

"I don't mean whistles and clicks," I said. "It was a voice inside my mind."

Mel and Shirley looked at each other. Mel laughed and shook his head. "Hey, get out of here."

"What did Fluffy say?" asked Shirley.

"'I've got you, dear. You're safe,'" I said.

"Hey, get out of here," said Mel again.

Shirley gave Mel a dirty look.

"Mel," she said. "Will you please let the young man talk?"

"Who's not letting him talk?" said Mel. "I'm letting him talk. I'm just saying 'Hey, get out of here.' That's all."

"Zack," said Shirley, "some people think that dolphins communicate with each other by some kind of ESP. It's just that I never heard of dolphins speaking to a person."

"Not till now," I said.

Chapter 2

Back in the motel cabin, I towelled off and started to put on some dry clothes. I thought about what had happened. Did a dolphin really talk to me? Weirder things than that have happened. But why me? Mel and Shirley had known Ralph and Fluffy for years. Wouldn't Fluffy have picked them instead? Had it just been in my mind?

I wanted to see if it would happen again. So instead of putting on dry clothes, I threw on my swimsuit.

When I got back to the pool, Mel and

Shirley were playing Scrabble again.

"Hey, Shirl, get out of here," Mel was saying. "That isn't a real word."

Shirley looked up and saw me. "Zack, it looks like you're ready for a real swim. Do you want to go to the beach?"

"Well," I said, "I was kind of wondering if I could maybe swim around with Ralph and Fluffy." That's when I looked over and saw that Ralph and Fluffy weren't in the pool. "Hey, where did they go?"

"Oh, the pool cleaners are coming. So we put the kids in the side pool for a while."

Shirley pointed to a smaller pool that was connected to the big one by a little underwater door.

"Hey, Zack," said Mel. "How's about taking a spin on a ride instead? We've got a couple that'll really knock your socks off!"

I doubted that their rides would knock

my socks off, even if I was wearing any. But I didn't want to hurt Mel's feelings. So I followed him to the Diving Dolphins ride.

It's like those kiddie airplane rides. The planes go around in circles, and you make them go up and down with a joystick. Well, this ride had dolphins instead of planes.

"Get ready for the ride of your life!" said Mel. Then he started the ride.

Frankly, I've been on scarier rides driving with my dad on the West Side Highway in New York. Mel and Shirley's place is probably a blast for three-year-olds, but Mel looked so excited, I couldn't let him down.

"Whoa!" I yelled. "This is great!"

I threw my hands in the air and let out a couple of screams. After about twenty minutes, Mel stopped the ride and I got out.

"Was that great or was that great?" said Mel.

"It was great," I said.

"I'd forgotten how nice it is to see kids enjoying the rides. Nobody's been on these for months," Shirley said sadly.

"You're not doing so great, huh?" I said.

"The big parks are trying to drive us little guys out of business," said Shirley. "They have lots of money to get the big rides. To get the big animal acts. And to run big ads. We can't really compete with them. If things don't get better soon, well, I'm afraid we're going to have to close."

Now Shirley looked like she was going to cry. I felt really sorry for them.

"If you had to close the park," I said, "what would happen to Ralph and Fluffy?"

"Oh, lots of people know about Ralph and Fluffy. How smart they are," Mel told me. "We've had lots of offers for them from the bigger parks. Especially from an awful man who calls himself Long John

Silverschnitzel. He owns a new theme park called Human Skull Island."

Oh, right! Human Skull Island. Dad and I had seen four or five huge billboards for it on the way to Mel and Shirley's place. It looked kind of cool. But I didn't say that to Mel and Shirley.

"That bum," said Mel, shaking his head. "I wouldn't sell him Ralph and Fluffy for all the tea in China."

"I don't blame you," I said. "I mean what would you do with that much tea anyway?"

"That's just an expression, dear," said Shirley. "We wouldn't sell Ralph and Fluffy to *anybody*. They're like children to us."

Just then a grubby green VW van pulled up to the front entrance of the park. Two guys with beards got out of it. One was tall and fat. The other was short and skinny.

"Look!" I said. "Customers!"

Mel and Shirley looked over at the van. "No, Zack," said Shirley. "Those are the pool cleaners, Horace and Boris."

We left the rides and walked back to the pool. Horace and Boris pulled out long poles with brushes and went to work. Mel and Shirley looked like they really wanted to finish their Scrabble game. So I went over to the smaller pool and watched Ralph and Fluffy.

They were swimming round and round, taking turns chasing each other. I wondered if they'd ever talk to me again. I waved at them. They turned over on their backs and waved their flippers.

"Ralph? Fluffy?" I said. "Can you understand me?"

They didn't look like they even heard me.

"If you can understand me," I said, "please say something. Anything at all."

Nothing. So it had to be one of two things. Either it had all been in my mind. Or else it only worked underwater. I wished Horace and Boris would finish so I could find out.

About fifteen minutes later, Horace and Boris let the dolphins back into the big pool. Ralph splashed them, but not in a playful way. Fluffy blew water from her blowhole all over them. I could tell Ralph and Fluffy didn't like the pool cleaners. And I could tell the pool cleaners didn't like the dolphins either.

"You think you're so clever," I heard Horace mutter. "Well, just you wait. You may not be around here much longer!"

Whoa, what did *that* mean? Was it some kind of threat? If Ralph and Fluffy would ever talk to me again, maybe I'd find out!

Chapter 3

"**Y**ow!" I yelled as I jumped into the big pool. The water was still pretty cold. Ralph and Fluffy were over on the far side of the pool. They were watching me closely. I swam over to them.

"Hi, guys," I said out loud.

They just continued to stare at me. Nothing. Not a word. I must have been imagining it. Maybe I swallowed too much chlorine or something when I fell in. But just to be sure, I dove underwater. So did the dolphins. Wow! They sure looked big.

Even bigger underwater. I wondered how much these guys weighed.

"**I'm 318 pounds,**" said a gruff voice inside my head.

"**And I'm 316,**" said a soft voice inside my head. "**I took off five pounds just this week.**"

"**What's happening?**" I thought. "**How can they read my mind?**"

"**How can you read *ours*?**"

"**Good point. The soft voice must be Fluffy's. The gruff one,**" I thought, "**was probably Ralph's.**"

"**Well, it sure isn't Flipper's,**" said the gruff voice.

"**You know,**" I said, "**once in science class I got an electric shock. And all day I could read everybody's thoughts. Including a goldfish and a piranha. So maybe that's it.**"

"**Maybe. But, dear, with us it only**

works if we're underwater. I guess thoughts travel better in water. Just like electricity."

By this time I felt like my lungs were about to burst. So I came up for air. There was Shirley peering down at me.

"Why don't you get out of the pool now, Zack?" said Shirley. "I don't want you to get too cold."

"I'm OK," I said. "Couldn't I stay in a little longer? I'm kind of in the middle of a conversation with Ralph and Fluffy."

Shirley nodded. Her eyes were very wide. I dove back underwater.

"So, kid," said the gruff voice. **"What do you know about us? Do you think we're fish or what?"**

"Uh, probably not. Aren't you air-breathing mammals?"

"Right," said Ralph. **"But do you know how smart we are?"**

"Well, uh, smarter than sharks?"

"Smarter than *sharks*?" Ralph roared. "Did you hear what he said, Fluff? Smarter than *sharks*! You kidding me? You know how big our brains are? As big as yours, kid. Bigger. You know how big a shark's brain is? As big as a Reese's Peanut Butter Cup! Plus we have sonar, kid. Do you know what sonar is?"

"Sort of."

"Well, do you or don't you?"

"Look, I didn't mean to insult you...."

"We send out a sound," said Ralph. "A clicking sound, OK? Like this: K-K-K-K-K-K-K-K. When it bounces off something like a fish and comes back to us, we can tell exactly how far away it is. How big it is. What it looks like. You think humans have sonar?"

"I guess not...."

"Well, you're wrong. Humans do have sonar. But you have to get it in a store, kid. We already have it in our heads, OK? We don't have to buy it at Radio Shack."

"Look, I'm sorry," I said after filling my lungs with air once more. "I really am. I had no idea how smart you guys are."

"You can say *that* again. Hey, we'd do *The New York Times* crossword puzzle if we could hold a pencil. For sure we could beat Mel and Shirley at Scrabble."

"You could?"

"Easy. Mel doesn't even know how to use his triple word scores."

"Sometimes," said Fluffy, "when Mel and Shirley leave out the Scrabble board, we play a few games. It's fun. Everything's fun here."

"You sure seem happy here," I thought.

"Oh yes. We love it, dear. Mel and Shirley are lovely. Even though Mel is always telling people to get out of places. But Horace and Boris are, well..."

"They're bad news, Fluff, OK? They're even dumber than sharks. K-K-K-K-K-K. Those pool cleaners' brains are probably about the size of a peanut M&M."

"What did Horace mean when he said you wouldn't be around much longer?"

"We're not sure. But they're up to something," said Fluffy. "I just hope they're not planning to set us free."

"Yeah," Ralph added. "Here, Mel and Shirley throw us a fish every time we do something cute. You think anybody in the ocean is handing out free fish for being cute?"

"I guess not."

"You know what it's like in the ocean, kid? Hunt, hunt, hunt. No time to relax. No time for Scrabble."

"Well, don't worry. Mel and Shirley wouldn't let anything happen to you."

Even underwater I could hear Shirley calling for me to get out of the pool. I waved good-bye and swam to the surface.

I hoped I was right when I said the dolphins had nothing to worry about. Frankly, I thought Horace and Boris were trouble. Big trouble.

"My, you certainly spent a long time in the pool," said Shirley as she helped me out of the water.

"Yeah," I said. "Ralph and Fluffy have a lot on their minds."

"Uh huh. And what did they, uh, tell you, dear?"

"Oh, lots of stuff. About sonar, and how

they really like it here. They love you and Mel. Only one thing worries them."

"What's that?"

"They're afraid of Horace and Boris."

Shirley studied my face.

"I see," she said. "And...how did they tell you this?"

"I already said. I heard their voices in my head."

"You're serious," said Shirley.

I nodded.

"Well then, I want to talk to them, too!" she said. "I'll be back in a jiffy."

A couple minutes later she came back out in one of those old-lady bathing suits with a skirt. And a big pink rubber swim cap with orange flowers on it.

"So what do I do now?" she asked.

"Put your head underwater and think," I said.

"I have so much to ask them! Is the pool

water too cold? Do they want to try a new kind of fish? Do they want to do more shows or less?"

She gave me a big smile and jumped in.

Five minutes later she climbed out, dripping wet.

"What did they tell you?" I asked.

"Nothing," she replied. "Not a peep. Are you *sure* they spoke to you, Zack?"

"I swear!" I said.

I could tell Shirley didn't believe me. I had to talk to Dad as soon as he got back from interviewing the orange. Dad and I have been through a lot together. He was with me the time I got stuck in a parallel universe. He was with me the time my orthodontist turned into a monster. He was with me the time I started turning into a cat.

Dad wouldn't have any problem believing I had had a conversation with dolphins.

Chapter 4

"I'm sorry but I'm just having a problem believing you had a conversation with dolphins," said Dad.

It was almost dinnertime. Dad and I were driving to a new restaurant called Pasta 'n' Pirates. Mel had gotten free dinner coupons in the mail, good for today only. So we were meeting Mel and Shirley there.

"Dad, why can't you believe me?" I asked. "You've been there when I went through things just as weird as this.

Weirder, even. Remember when I started turning into a cat? Or when I made a clone of myself, and it started making more little clones all over the place?"

"Of course I remember."

"Then why can't you believe I had an ordinary everyday conversation with a couple of ordinary everyday dolphins?"

"You have a point there, Zack," Dad said with a sigh. "All right, let's say this is true. And let's say Horace and Boris are up to something. What can we do about it?"

"What about going to the cops?" I said.

"And say what? That a couple of dolphins told you they were afraid two guys might set them free?"

"I see the problem," I said. "I guess not."

Just then we pulled up to the restaurant. Outside there was a black flag with a skull and two crossed forks on it.

Mel and Shirley were already inside. It was fixed up to look like a pirate ship. The sounds of splashing waves came over a loudspeaker. The floor even moved up and down like we were on a ship in rough water.

Mel and Shirley waved to us, and we sat down at the table. A minute later this really weird-looking guy came over. He was wearing a pirate's hat, a curly black mustache, and a black eye patch. He had a sword on his belt and a parrot on his shoulder.

"Avast there, mates," he said. "Welcome to me new restaurant. What can I get ye?"

"This is *your* place?" said Mel, throwing down his napkin.

"Who's this?" I asked.

"Long John Silverschnitzel," said Shirley. Her face was all red. "The man who tried to buy Ralph and Fluffy for Human Skull Island!"

"Now, mates," said Long John. "I'm

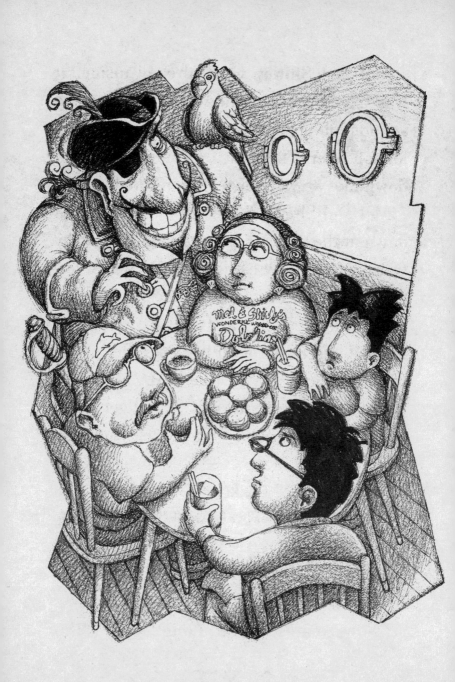

hoisting the flag of truce! I'll not be needing those dolphins after all. Human Skull Island is drawing in more crowds than Captain Kidd's hanging. I want to patch things up. That's why I sent you the coupons. I want to treat you to dinner."

Mel and Shirley looked at each other.

"I guess we can let bygones be bygones," said Shirley.

"Hang me from a yardarm if them ain't the sweetest words," said Long John. Then he waved at a waiter. "Smee, you take good care of these fine people."

After Long John left, Shirley said, "Maybe Long John's a good man after all."

"Get out of here," was all Mel said.

I have to admit we had a good time. The service was very slow. But Smee kept bringing us extra stuff like shark-shaped cookies.

"Compliments of the Cap'n," he told us.

It was pretty late by the time we got back. I was in the bathroom, brushing my teeth.

That's when I heard the scream out by the dolphin pool. It was pretty loud.

I dropped my toothbrush. Dad and I raced outside.

Shirley was standing next to the dolphin pool. She looked really upset.

"Shirley," said Dad. "What's wrong?"

"They're gone!" she cried. "Ralph and Fluffy—they've been kidnapped!"

~⌐~

Mel was on the phone to the police.

"Their names are Ralph and Fluffy," he said. "They were last seen in the pool at 6 P.M." There was a pause as he listened to the next question. "I guess they each weigh about 320 pounds," he answered.

"Actually, they weigh 318 and 316," I said, but Mel wasn't listening to me.

"Well, they're sort of grayish," said Mel.

"What were they wearing? Nothing." There was a longer pause. I don't think the guy at the police station realized Mel was talking about missing dolphins. He probably thought Mel was reporting two very large, naked people with grayish skin.

Mel finally got off the phone.

"The police can't send anyone over tonight," he said. "But a detective will be here tomorrow morning."

"I'm positive Horace and Boris are behind this," I told Mel and Shirley. "The dolphins were afraid they were planning something like this."

But there was nothing to do, except wait for the detective to come in the morning.

Dad had already left for the orange grove when Detective Rosenblum arrived at nine on the dot. She was short—even shorter than Boris. But she looked really tough.

I told Detective Rosenblum what I'd heard Horace mutter to the dolphins. She nodded and wrote that in a little notebook.

As soon as Horace and Boris showed up, she started giving them the third degree.

She walked over to Horace.

"All right, Horace," said Detective Rosenblum. "What have you and Boris done with the individuals known as Ralph and Fluffy?"

Horace shook his head. "Nothing."

"Nothing?" said Detective Rosenblum. "But isn't it true you told the individuals in question that they might not be around here much longer?"

Horace looked at Boris.

"I might have said that," said Horace. "I can't remember."

"Excuse me, officer," said Boris in a high, squeaky voice.

"Yes, Boris?" said Detective Rosenblum.

"When were the dolphins kidnapped?"

"Between 6 and 9 P.M. yesterday evening," said Detective Rosenblum.

"Well, between 6 and 9 P.M. yesterday evening," said Boris, "Horace and I were at our other job."

"What's your other job?"

"We test underarm deodorants at the Stink-No-More Deodorant factory," said Boris. "We're sniffers."

"You're what?"

"People put different deodorants under their arms," said Boris. "We sniff to see how well they work."

"I see," said Detective Rosenblum. "And someone at the factory will swear that you were there yesterday evening?"

"Oh yes," said Boris.

"And you had absolutely no plan to kidnap or do bodily harm to the individuals known as Ralph and Fluffy?"

"Uh, well, no, not really," said Boris.

"Excuse me?" said the Detective.

"Boris..." said Horace.

"To be perfectly honest," said Boris, "we did have a plan a *little* like that...."

"Boris..." said Horace a little louder.

"But we never got a chance to do it, I swear," said Boris. "Because somebody else beat us to the punch."

"Boris!" said Horace.

"What?" said Boris.

"Shut *up!*" said Horace.

"Are you gentlemen finished?" asked Detective Rosenblum.

"Pretty much," said Boris.

"Then why don't we drive down to Stink-No-More so I can check out this cockamamy story of yours."

The pool cleaners followed her to her police car. I wished Detective Rosenblum had put handcuffs on them. But she didn't.

Chapter 5

Well, what do you know? Horace and Boris were telling the truth. The head sniffer at the Stink-No-More factory said they really had been sniffing armpits there between the hours of 6 and 9 P.M. yesterday evening. So Detective Rosenblum had to let them go.

"I'd advise you folks to stick close to a phone," she said to us. "In case some bozo calls with a ransom demand."

So we did. Dad was still over at the orange grove working on his story. But

Mel, Shirley, and I hung around the front office.

It was sad seeing the empty dolphin pool. Mel tried to get Shirley to play a game of Scrabble. He thought maybe it would take her mind off things.

"Mel, how can I think about triple word scores at a time like this?" she asked.

"I know," said Mel, shaking his head sadly. "Shirl, I still think it had to be those two bums. Who else could it be?"

"It could have been anyone," said Shirley. "It could have been the Mafia."

"Get out of here," said Mel. "What would the Mafia want with Ralph and Fluffy?"

"I'm so upset, I don't even know what I'm saying," said Shirley.

I felt really bad for both Shirley and Mel. I also felt really bad for Ralph and Fluffy. Where were they? How much money did somebody think they could get for two dolphins? And then I went back to the idea that whoever took Ralph and Fluffy had set them free in the ocean. Maybe somebody thought they were doing the dolphins a favor. But it wasn't such a favor. As Ralph himself said, nobody in the ocean was handing out free fish for being cute.

"You know," I said, "Ralph and Fluffy were afraid somebody would set them free in the ocean. If that's what happened, maybe I could contact them."

"How could you do that?" asked Mel.

"I could go into the ocean myself and see if I could send them a message somehow," I said. "Thoughts travel better in water. Just like electricity."

"Who told you that?" asked Shirley.

"Fluffy did," I said.

I bet you can guess what Mel said next....

"Get out of here!" said Mel.

But Shirley wanted to try. And Mel would do anything for Shirley. So the three of us drove to the ocean.

It was a nice hot day. I waded out into the water.

"Good luck!" said Mel.

"Don't go too far out!" said Shirley.

The water wasn't even up to my knees. Shirley was a lot like my Grandma Leah!

When I got out deep enough, I held my nose. Then I went under. I started sending out messages: **"Attention, Ralph and Fluffy. Attention, Ralph and Fluffy. This is Zack. Do you copy? Come in, please!"** I wasn't too sure what "Do you copy?" meant. But they say that on TV cop shows and I thought it sounded good.

Nothing at all. I came up for air.

"Do you hear anything?" Shirley called.

"Not yet," I said.

"I don't understand why they aren't answering," said Mel. "Are you sure you're doing it the right way?"

"What's the right way?" I said.

"How should *I* know?" said Mel. "*You're* the psychic."

Boy! A little while ago they didn't even believe I could talk to dolphins. And now Mel thought I wasn't doing it right? Give me a break! But I could see how upset they were. So all I said was, "I'll try again."

So I did: **"Attention, Ralph. Attention, Fluffy. This is Zack calling. If you can hear me, please answer now!"**

And then, just as I was ready to call it quits, I thought I heard something. It was kind of fuzzy at first. But the sounds were getting louder:

"Zack! I read you. Repeat: I read you."

"Ralph? Fluffy? Is that you?"

"No, it's Tiffany."

"Uh, Tiffany," I said. "Are you a dolphin?"

"Of course. An Atlantic bottle-nose."

"Well," I said, "I'm trying to reach two dolphins named Ralph and Fluffy. They were kidnapped. I thought maybe they were taken to the ocean. Have you seen any new dolphins around?"

"Nope. But I'll get in touch with Ellsworth. He's only a porpoise. But he knows *everybody*."

Tiffany asked if I could give her a couple of minutes to talk to Ellsworth. I said sure. I waded back to Mel and Shirley and told them I might be on to something. In five minutes I went back underwater. Tiffany was waiting for me.

"Bad news, Zack. Ellsworth is gone. His cousin Warren told me."

"Gone? What do you mean gone?"

"Poor Ellsworth. He's been taken to Human Skull Island. That's three of my friends so far who've been kidnapped by that lousy fake pirate!"

Aha! That was it! That's why Long John Silverschnitzel sent Mel free dinner coupons. Just so he'd have time to kidnap the dolphins while we were eating! I splashed through the water to Mel and Shirley.

"Mel, we have to go to Human Skull Island right away!" I shouted. "I think that's where Long John Silverschnitzel has taken Ralph and Fluffy!"

"What makes you think that, dear?" asked Shirley.

"Tiffany told me," I said.

"Who's Tiffany, dear?"

"She's an Atlantic bottle-nosed dolphin. She said Ellsworth, who's a porpoise, might know...." I stopped. "It's a long story. I'll tell you on the way. But now let's go!"

Chapter 6

On our way to Human Skull Island we picked up Detective Rosenblum. Then we made another stop to get Dad.

The world's largest orange was at a little orange grove, still hanging on the tree.

I spotted Dad. He was talking to a man in a green jumpsuit.

"So would an orange this size have a lot more seeds than a normal one?" Dad was asking in this really serious voice. "Or would the seeds just be bigger?"

"Dad!" I shouted. "I think I found out

where they've taken Ralph and Fluffy!"

Dad immediately ended his interview. We all squeezed into Mel's car. I was all scrunched up in the back seat. And something was poking my butt. I reached down and felt around. It was a Scrabble tile. The letter G. There was a whole Scrabble set on the shelf behind my head.

Before long we were at Human Skull Island. The first thing you see as you get near it is this mountain of white rock. It really does look like a human skull. Mostly because it has two big caves near the top, which look like eyeholes.

If I were going there alone at night, I'd be scared. Especially if it was raining and there was lightning and thunder and wind that sounded like screaming zombies. But it was daytime and the sun was shining. And I was there with a bunch of people including a cop. So I wasn't scared at all. Hardly at all.

As soon as we got out of Mel's car, Long John Silverschnitzel came up to us.

"Avast there, mates!" he said cheerily. But he pulled on his eye patch nervously. "And what can we do for ye? Free passes, perhaps?"

"We've come for Ralph and Fluffy," said Shirley.

"Shiver me timbers," said Long John Silverschnitzel. "And who might Ralph and Fluffy be?"

"Our dolphins, that's who, you big creep!" said Mel. "And get out of here with that fake accent. I happen to know you come from New Jersey."

Long John gave Mel a long look.

"No, Mel, *you* get out of here," said Long John. He had dropped his pirate accent. "Or else I'm calling the cops."

"Mr. Silverschnitzel, I *am* the cops," said Detective Rosenblum, stepping forward.

She opened her jacket. Inside you could see her badge and her shoulder holster. "And we would like to see the individuals known as Ralph and Fluffy."

Long John looked a little shaken.

"Uh, we don't have anybody here with that name, Officer," he said.

"Mr. Silverschnitzel, do you have dolphins here with any name whatsoever?" she asked.

"We might have some dolphins here," said Long John. "We might not. I don't really remember."

"Perhaps this will refresh your memory," said Detective Rosenblum.

She took out photos of Ralph and Fluffy and shoved them in his face. He looked at them and shrugged.

"No more games. Take us to the dolphins, Silverschnitzel," said the detective. "Now!"

Long John led the way into one of the eyehole caves. It was pretty dark in there. But in the water you could see something moving. Dolphins! Lots of them.

"Ralph? Fluffy? Are you there?" Shirley shouted.

Long John held her back.

Two dolphins poked their heads out of the water. They waved their flippers at us.

"Ralph! Fluffy! It's you!" yelled Mel.

"These dolphins are not who you think they are," Long John said. "They're mine. Every single one of them. I have papers to prove it."

He fished in his jacket and came out with a bunch of papers. It was too dark to read in the cave. Long John lit a torch.

Detective Rosenblum looked at the papers. Then she turned to Mel and Shirley.

"I hate to say this," she said. "But these papers look pretty convincing."

Long John had a very pleased look on his face.

"But he's lying!" said Shirley. "Two of those dolphins aren't his. They're ours!"

"I want to believe you," said Detective Rosenblum. "But how can you prove it?"

"How should *I* know?" said Mel.

"I have an idea!" I said. Everybody turned to look at me. "I'll be back in a minute."

I ran to the car and got the Scrabble set. Then I ran back to the eyehole cave.

"*Now* you want to play Scrabble?" said Shirley.

"Just watch," I said. I sure hoped this would work. If not, how would Mel and Shirley ever get their dolphins back? I opened the Scrabble box and dumped the tiles on the floor of the cave.

"What on earth is he doing?" asked Long John.

I took off my shoes, my shirt, and my jeans. I still had my swimsuit on underneath. I started to get into the water.

"Hey!" said Long John. "Where do you think you're going, kid?"

"I just want to get into the pool to talk to the dolphins," I said.

"Well, I won't allow it!" said Long John.

"I will, however," said Detective Rosenblum. "Go ahead, Zack."

I slipped into the water. Ralph and Fluffy seemed really glad to see me.

"Hi, guys," I said. "Are you OK?"

"We're OK. But we want to go home."

"Good. You will. But first we have to prove to Detective Rosenblum you are who we say you are. Still remember how to play Scrabble?"

"Of course."

"Good. Then use the Scrabble tiles to spell out something convincing."

I surfaced and got out of the water. Ralph and Fluffy swam to the edge of the pool. They poked their heads out of the water. They stuck their beaks into the pile of Scrabble tiles. They started pushing them around. Everyone moved forward to watch.

So did I. I looked at what they had spelled out: IM RALPH IM FLUFY LONG JOHN IS A CROOK.

Long John looked like he'd been punched in the stomach. Shirley, Mel, Dad, and I all shouted for joy.

"These dolphins are brilliant," said Dad. "But Fluffy isn't too good a speller, is she?"

"She's a great speller," I said. "But there are only two F's in a Scrabble set."

Detective Rosenblum took out a pair of handcuffs and snapped them on Long John Silverschnitzel.

"You have the right to remain silent," she said. "And, frankly, I'd advise it."

Chapter 7

So Ralph and Fluffy came back home. Ellsworth and the other dolphins that Long John took from the ocean were set free. And Long John Silverschnitzel went to jail.

Detective Rosenblum did a little more investigating and found out Horace and Boris *had* planned to kidnap Ralph and Fluffy. I won't even tell you what they wanted to do to them. Let's just say that Mel and Shirley fired them—right away.

There've been a few other changes around Mel & Shirley's Wonderful World of Dolphins. Some stories about the kidnapping ran in the papers. Once people found out about Ralph and Fluffy, the Scrabble-playing dolphins, crowds started lining up outside the park to see them.

Now, instead of a neon sign on the roof of the motel, Mel and Shirley have a state-of-the-art digital marquee at the park entrance. And all the billboards along the turnpike for Human Skull Island have been replaced with ones for Mel & Shirley's Wonderful World of Dolphins.

I'm back in New York now. But I still call Mel and Shirley every once in a while. And I've sent Ralph and Fluffy a couple of postcards. I didn't write them. I glued Scrabble tiles onto pieces of cardboard. It's not the easiest way to talk to somebody, but it's better than nothing.

The next time I'm in Florida, we'll have a lot of catching up to do.

What else happens to Zack?
Find out in

Now You See Me....
Now You Don't

"**Z**ack, you look very pale." Dad peered at me closely. "Well, not exactly pale. You actually seem to be...fading," he said. "As in becoming transparent."

"What?"

I ran to the bathroom and looked in the mirror. Dad was right. I did look kind of see-through—sort of cloudy the way ghosts look in movies. "Oh no!" I said. "The disappearing ink! Could it be?"

THE ZACK FILES™

OUT-OF-THIS-WORLD FAN CLUB!

Looking for even more info on all the strange, otherworldly happenings going on in *The Zack Files*? Get the inside scoop by becoming a member of *The Zack Files* Out-Of-This-World Fan Club! Just send in the form below and we'll send you your *Zack Files* Out-Of-This-World Fan Club kit including an official fan club membership card, a really cool *Zack Files* magnet, and a newsletter featuring excerpts from Zack's upcoming paranormal adventures, supernatural news from around the world, puzzles, and more! And as a member you'll continue to receive the newsletter six times a year! The best part is—it's all free!

✂ --

Yes! I want to check out *The Zack Files* Out-Of-This-World Fan Club!

name: _____ age: _____

address: _____

city/town: _____ state: ___ zip: _____

Send this form to: Penguin Putnam Books for
Young Readers
Mass Merchandise Marketing
Dept. ZACK
345 Hudson Street
New York, NY 10014